ANGEL
OF
DEATH

BRENTON FIFER

Copyright © 2020 by Brenton Fifer.

All rights reserved. No part of this book may be reproduced in any form or by any electronic or mechanical means, including information storage and retrieval systems, without permission in writing from the publisher, except by reviewers, who may quote brief passages in a review.

This publication contains the opinions and ideas of its author. It is intended to provide helpful and informative material on the subjects addressed in the publication. The author and publisher specifically disclaim all responsibility for any liability, loss, or risk, personal or otherwise, which is incurred as a consequence, directly or indirectly, of the use and application of any of the contents of this book.

WRITERS REPUBLIC L.L.C.
515 Summit Ave. Unit R1
Union City, NJ 07087, USA

Website: *www.writersrepublic.com*
Hotline: *1-877-656-6838*
Email: *info@writersrepublic.com*

Ordering Information:
Quantity sales. Special discounts are available on quantity purchases by corporations, associations, and others. For details, contact the publisher at the address above.

Library of Congress Control Number:	2020921056
ISBN-13: 978-1-64620-707-7	[Paperback Edition]
978-1-64620-701-5	[Digital Edition]

Rev. date: 11/03/2020

The Angel of Death is a creepy story about an old wooden box found during the demolition of an ancient church.

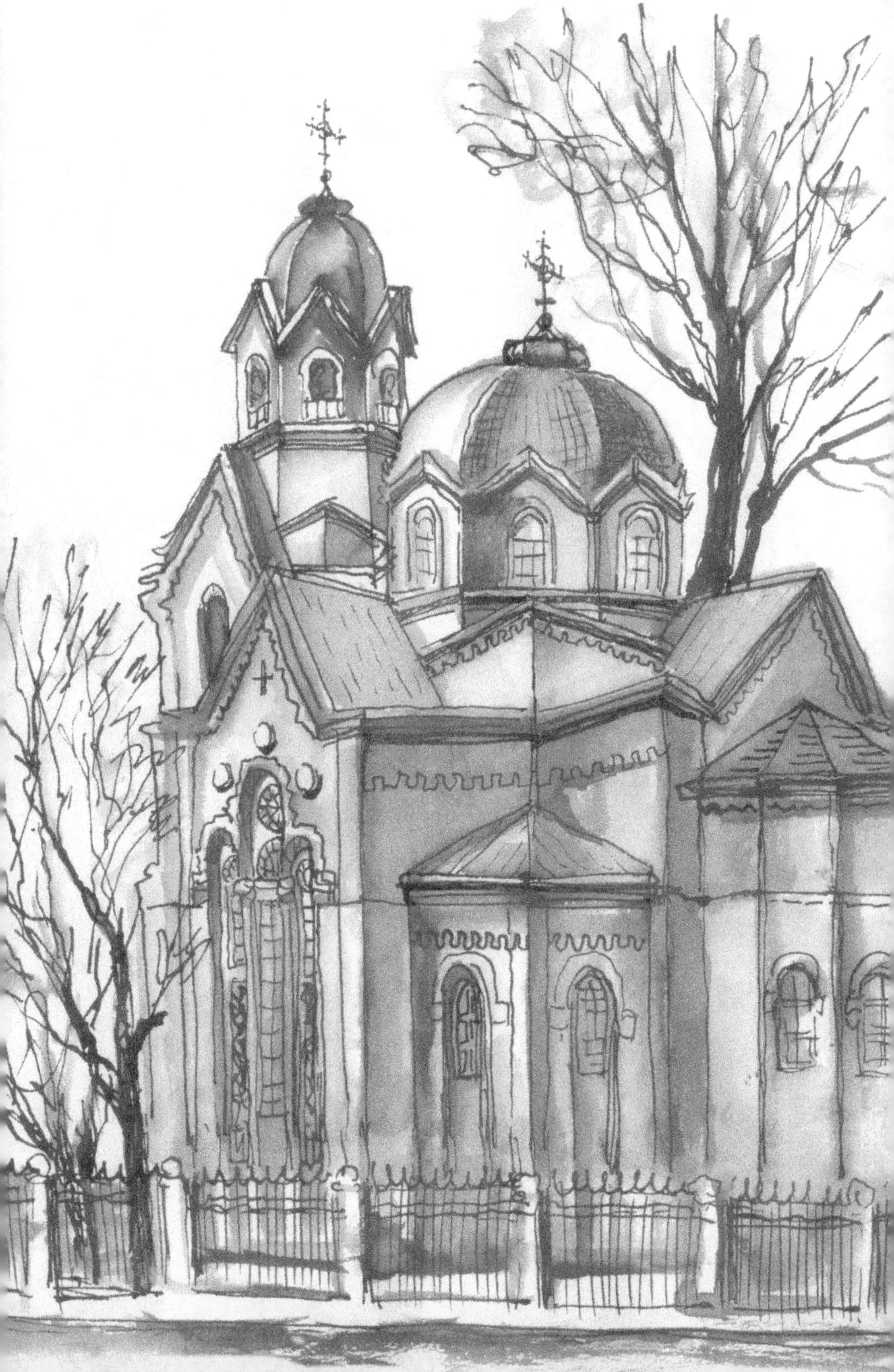

BRENTON FIFER   ANGEL OF DEATH

I work for a construction company and a few days ago, we were hired by a Catholic priest to do some renovations on an old church. While we were tearing down a wall, we found a small recess behind it. It was in a tiny room that had no entrance, as if it had been sealed off from the rest of the building. Inside, there was a long, black wooden box.

The box was about two meters long and very old. The wood was damp and rotten. There was something written on the side, but it was too worn and faded to make out. The box was nailed tightly shut and there didn't seem to be any way of opening it.

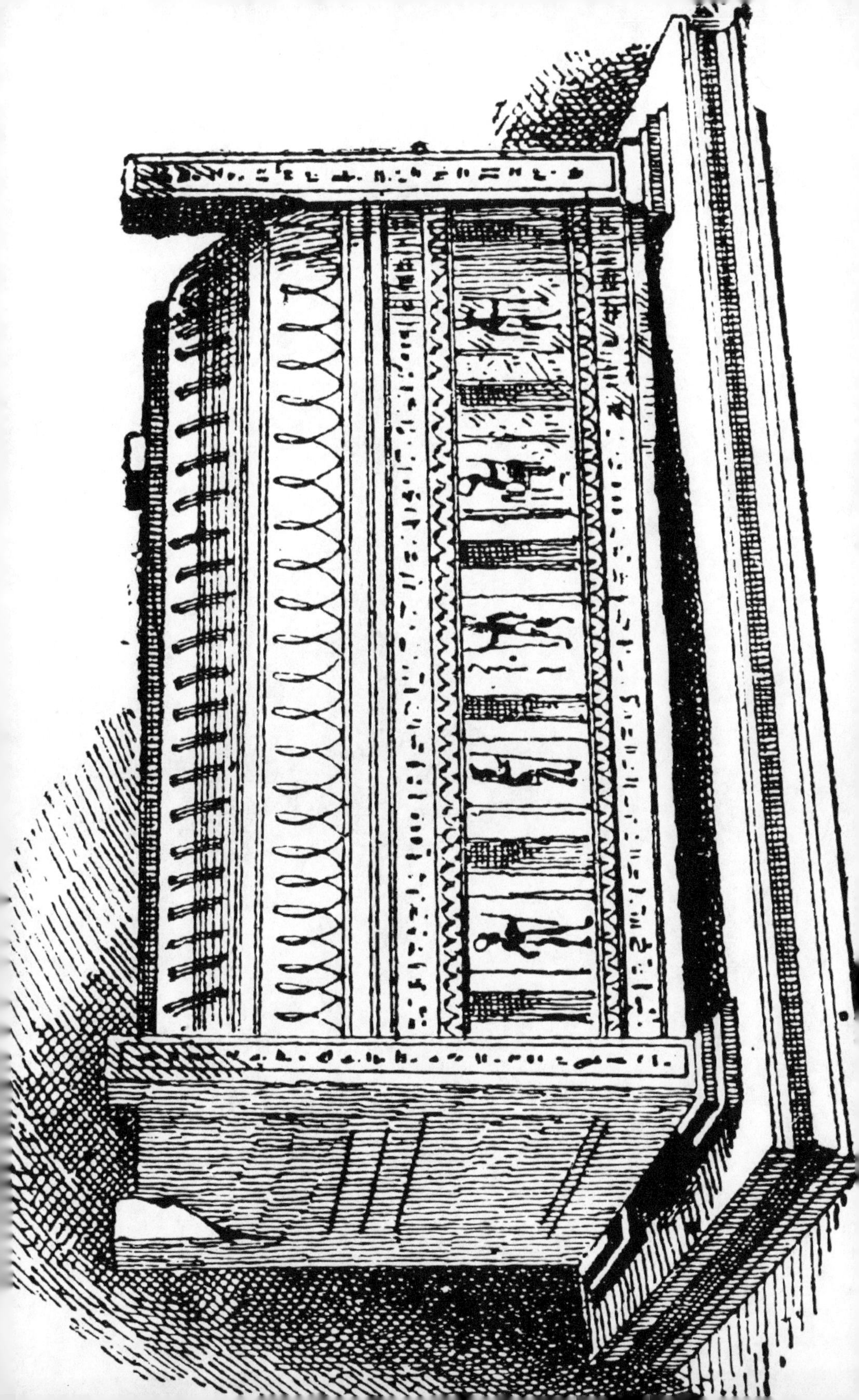

When I showed it to our boss, he told me to contact the priest and tell him about it. When I managed to get the priest on the phone and described the box to him, he became silent for a long time. Then, he told me he would come over in the morning and deal with it. In the meantime, he asked me to leave it somewhere safe.

I carried the box into the church and left it in a corner. I figured it would be safe there overnight, since the church was not in use. By that time, it was almost evening, so I packed up my things and went home.

The next day, when I arrived for work, my boss came hurrying over.

"About that box you found," he said. "There's a problem. Last night, two of the night watchmen came across it and... you're not going to believe this... the morons went and opened it."

I hurried into the church and found the two night watchmen sitting on the ground. My co-workers were standing around them. I suddenly had a very bad feeling in my stomach. Beside them, the wooden box lay open.

The priest was standing there, shaking his head.

"I warned you," he said. "I warned you not to open it. It's too soon."

"What's wrong with them?" I asked, pointing to the night watchmen.

"They haven't said a word since we got here," said my boss. "It's like they can't even hear us."

"You should bring them to the hospital," said the priest. "Although, it's probably already too late..."

Then, I walked over and peered into the wooden box. I was shocked to see that it contained a body. It was the mummified remains of what looked like a human being. However, it was unlike any human being I had ever laid eyes on. The strange

thing was, it had two heads. Both faces were hideously deformed. Even stranger, it had four arms. Two left arms and two right arms. It was the most baffling mutation I had ever seen.

Whatever it was, it really looked terrifying.

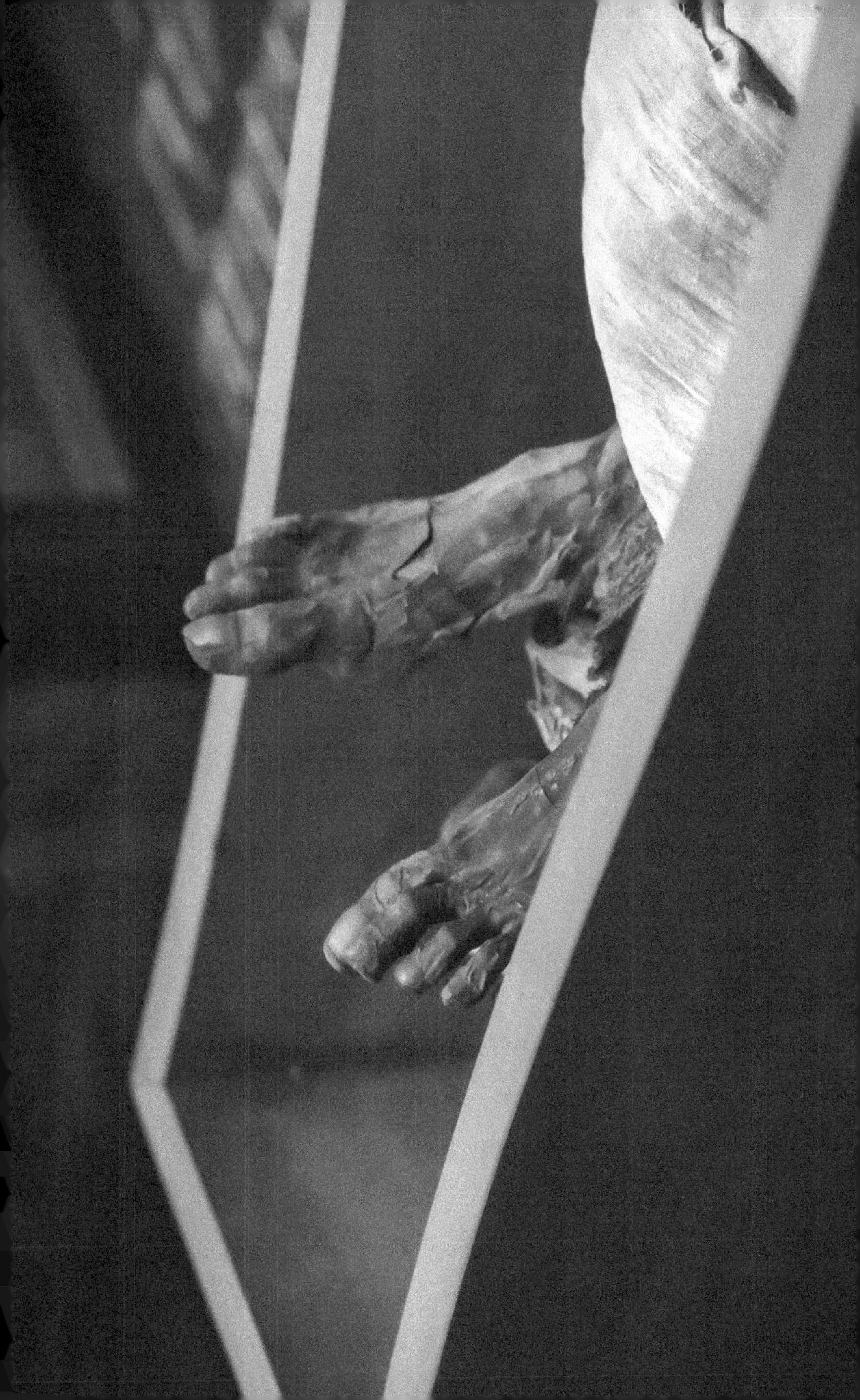

I could see that my co-workers were very disturbed. To calm them down, the priest went around the church, clutching his rosary beads, sprinkling holy water on everything and reciting something in Latin. The night watchmen were taken to the hospital and we debated whether we should call the police.

The priest loaded the wooden box into the boot of his car. Then, he stopped and hung his head. He couldn't even look us in the eyes.

"I am sorry for all of you," he said sadly. "You don't have long to live…"

With that, he drove off and we were left scratching our heads.

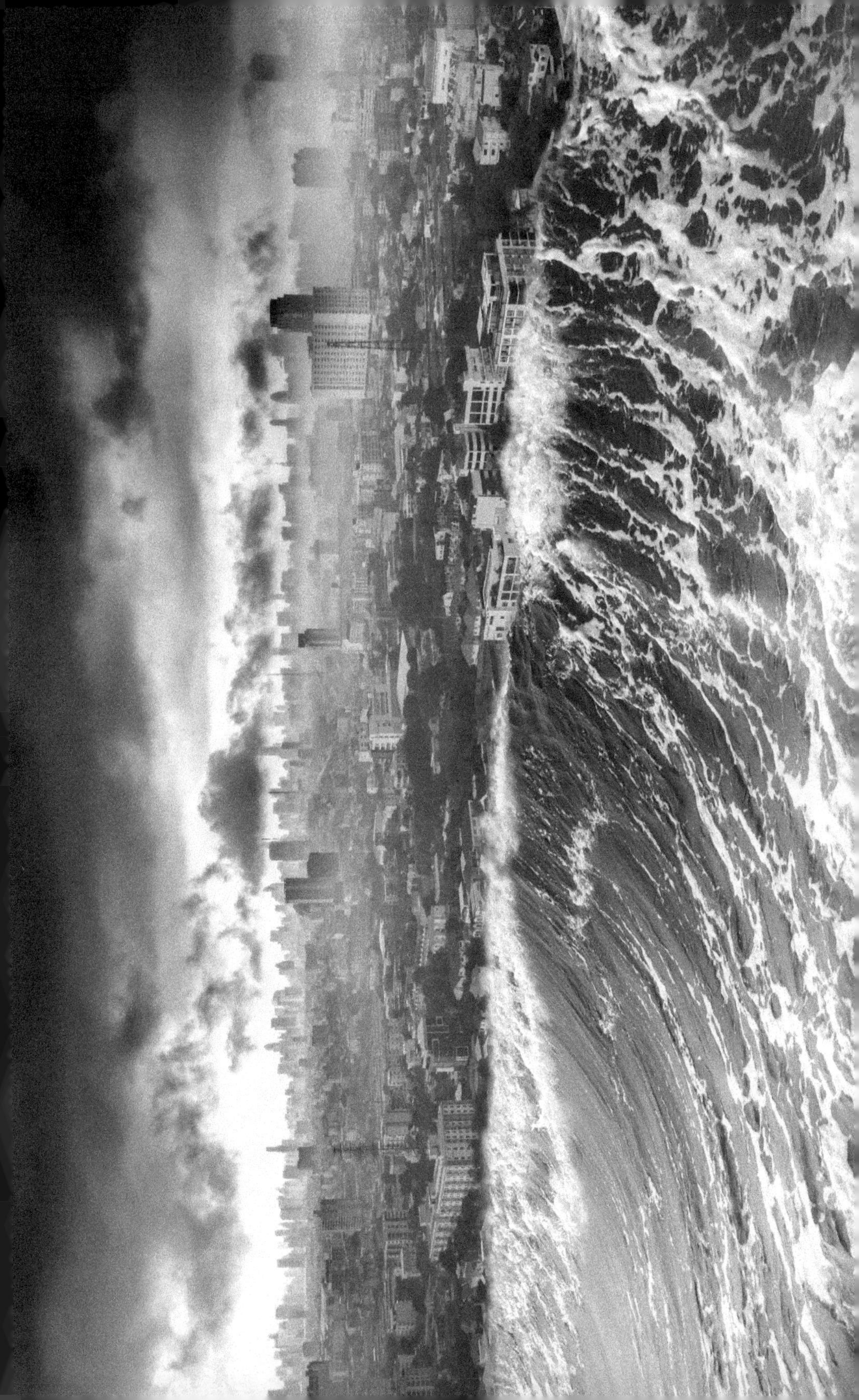

In the days that followed, strange things began to happen. We heard that one of the night watchmen died in hospital. He had a heart attack, even though he was only in his early 30s. The other was transferred to a mental institution. Three of my co-workers came down with a mysterious illness and had to be hospitalized.

That evening, as I was leaving work, I tripped on some rubble and tore a ligament in my leg. It meant that I couldn't work and was forced to recover at home.

I had too much time on my hands and strange thoughts were swirling around my head. I couldn't get the words of the priest out of my mind. Today, I tried calling him several times and eventually, he answered his phone.

We talked for over two hours and he told me a lot. Perhaps he told me too much:

Me: I have to know. What exactly was that thing?

Him: He died many years ago. At one time, he was a human being... or I should say, two human beings... two deformed children. They came from a small village in the South, but their parents were extremely poor and they ended up selling them to a slave dealer. Somehow, they ended up being put on display in a traveling freak show that toured the country.

Me: So... I don't understand. If they were two people... How did they become one person? Do you mean they were Siamese twins?

Him: Are you sure you want me to tell you about this?

Me: Yes, I really want to know.

Him: Good, good... I wasn't going to tell you everything... But what harm can it do? No, they were not Siamese twins. They were not born that way. However, they did have severely deformed faces. At the time, there was a religious cult... they acted in secret... you'll have to forgive me for not saying the name of the cult aloud... but it has to do with devil worship...

Their leader was a man by the name of Mononobe Tengoku... He went to the freak show and paid large sums of money for... specimens... peculiar aberrations... He bought the twins, you see, for his collection...

Me: What did he want them for?

Him: There is a legend about a certain occult ritual. It states that it is possible for someone to create a very powerful curse... They say that if you put two poisonous insects in a jar, they will fight to the death and you can use the one that survives to make the curse more potent... something about combining the live one with the dead one... Well, Tengoku used that method on human beings. Taking that little story about the curse as inspiration, Tengoku decided to try it with people... He conducted his terrible experiments in a hidden room in the basement... He left the twins alone in that room without food or water...

Me: How long were they locked in the room?

Him: Long enough for one to eventually kill and cannibalize the other. Quite some time, I imagine.

Me: I would rather not imagine such things...

Him: But the cruelty didn't end there. The last one left alive in that room was taken out and Tengoku set about combining him with his dead brother... He had no pity for them... He didn't see them as human beings... For him, they were just a tool, a means to an end... Using crude surgery, he removed the head and arms of the dead twin and sewed them to the body of the surviving twin... That is how this thing was created...

Me: He created a monstrosity on purpose?

Him: Tengoku did not regard it as that. He was completely enraptured with what he had created. In the time of legends, there was a mythic beast called a Ryoumensukuna. It was a two-headed, four-armed monster. Tengoku named his creation after that legend. He and his followers worshipped it like an evil deity. They locked it in a room and starved it to death. Then, they performed dark occult rituals in honor of it...

Me: I see...

Him: Tengoku used the Ryoumensukuna as a sort of cursed talisman, if you will. He believed that he had created an unparalleled evil, one that could kill large numbers of people... An angel of death...

Me: Who was the target of the curse?

Him: Every living thing in this world... Every single person on earth...

Me: What? Was Tengoku crazy or something?

Him: That's definitely possible. The curse is very powerful. The Ryoumensukuna began turning up at the site of natural disasters. Wherever there was an earthquake, a flood, a fire, a tsunami... In the days leading up to the disaster, the Ryoumensukuna was found. The followers of this cult are still alive... still transporting the remains of the Ryoumensukuna... causing death and destruction in its wake...

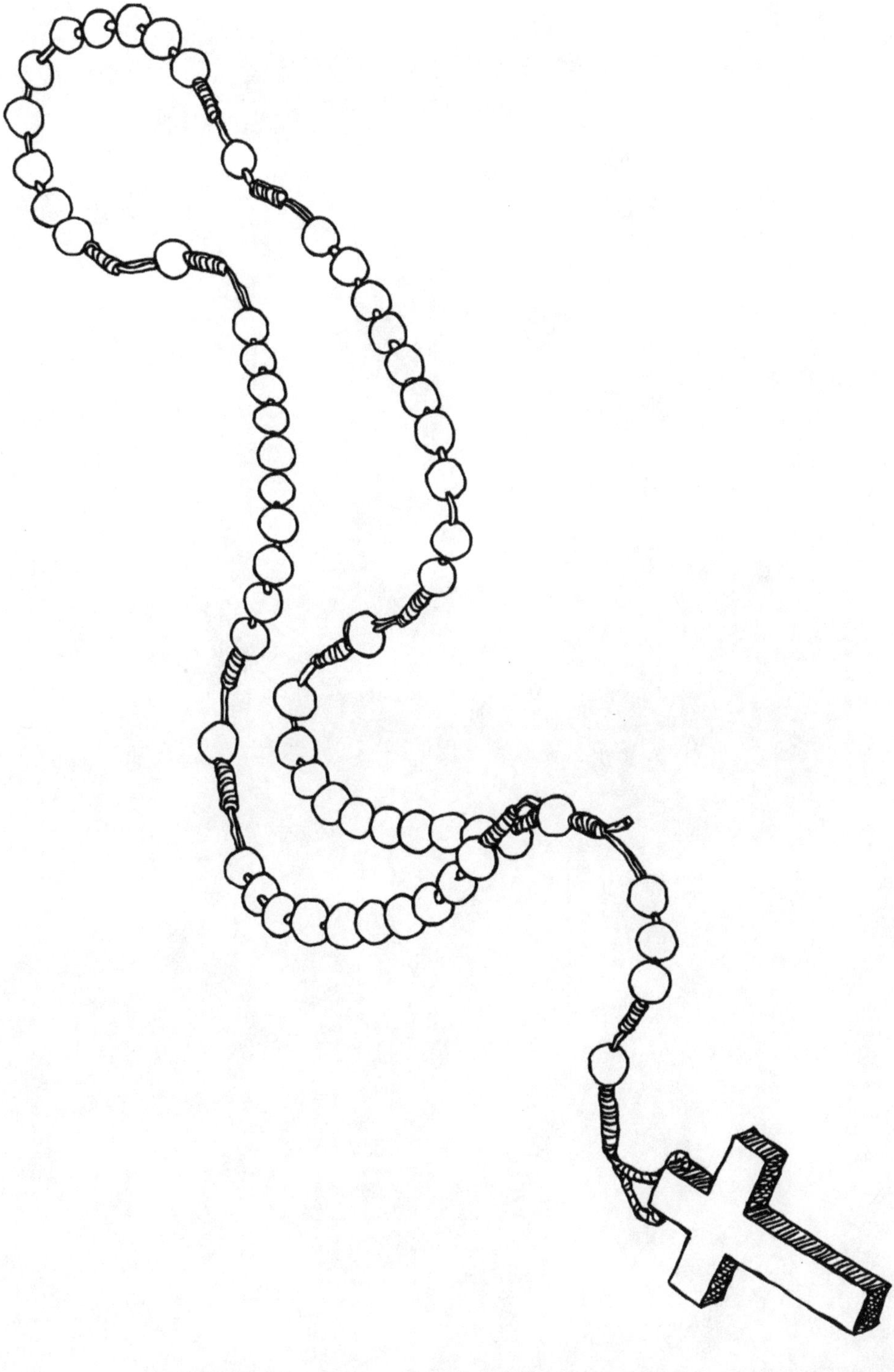

Me: You mean, every disaster in the last 100 years had been caused by this Ryoumensukuna?

Him: Exactly.

Me: This is unbelievable! The cult has branches all over the world?

Him: They do. Their goal is the destruction of every living thing in this world.

Me: But this couldn't be true... It's just a coincidence, right?

Him: That the Ryoumensukuna has appeared before every disaster that has occurred in the last 100 years? Well, it would have to be a very amazing coincidence...

Me: Where is the Ryoumensukuna now?

Him: Somewhere safe... until it is needed again...

Me: You... you are bringing it somewhere else?

Him: In the future, yes.

Me: You're a member of this cult aren't you?

Him: I was wondering if you'd ask me that...

Me: You are, aren't you? Are you crazy or something?

Him: That's definitely possible.

Me: What is going to happen?

Him: I don't know precisely. The Ryoumensukuna determines what happens. We can only watch from afar and revel in the wanton death and destruction...

Me: Why have you told me so much?

Him: I'm sorry, but it doesn't matter. You see, you won't be alive much longer and anyway, who would believe you?

Me: But how can you do this? It's evil! It's meaningless slaughter! What goal does it serve? What could be the point?
Him: Let us leave it at that. Don't call here again.

After he hung up the phone, I began wracking my brain, trying to figure out what I should do. I couldn't warn anybody. He was right, no one would believe me. I immediately booked a flight out of the country. At least I could try and save my own skin.

I'm on my way to the airport right now. I hope I can get away in time. I hope it's not too late.

If you are watching the news and you see reports of a disaster in the next few days, one that kills a large number of people, then you will know what caused it.

Just pray that this Ryoumensukuna doesn't turn up in your country...